CL

05 F

WITHDRAWN

D0581914

a ballet

Using this book

Ladybird's *talkabouts* are ideal for encouraging children to talk about what they see. Bold colourful pictures and simple questions help to develop early learning skills — such as matching, counting and detailed observation.

Look at this book with your child. First talk about the pictures yourself, and point out things to look at. Let your child take his* time. With encouragement, he will start to join in, talking about the familiar things in the pictures. Help him to count objects, to look for things that match, and to talk about what is going on in the picture stories.

To avoid the clumsy use of he/she, the child is referred to as 'he', **talkabouts** *are suitable for both boys and girls.*

Published by Ladybird Books Ltd
80 Strand London WC2R ORL
A Penguin Company

3 5 7 9 10 8 6 4

© LADYBIRD BOOKS MMIII

LADYBIRD and the device of a ladybird are trademarks of Ladybird Books Ltd
All rights reserved. No part of this publication may be reproduced, stored in a retrieval system, or
transmitted in any form or by any means, electronic, mechanical, photocopying, recording or otherwise,
without the prior consent of the copyright owner.

Printed in Italy

talkabout
Busy town

written by Lorraine Horsley
illustrated by Alex Ayliffe

Ladybird

What is happening here in Busy Town?
Talk about the picture.

6

7

Can you find these in the shoe shop?

Which pair would you choose?

Decorating the bedroom.
Tell the story.

Jack and his mum are shopping for new clothes.

Which clothes are too big?
Which clothes are just right?

13

Shiny red peppers and sweet green grapes...
What other fruits and vegetables can you see?

How many carrots
can you count?

Find another...

banana

tomato

lettuce

17

There's so much to do in Busy Town...
What are the people doing?

Pretty pink roses smell so sweet...
Talk about what you can see
in the flower shop.

What colours are the flowers?
Which is your favourite?

Can you find these toys in the toy shop?

Which toy
would you like?

What happens at the supermarket?
Tell the story.

3

4

At the pet shop there are big and small pets.
Who has fur and who has fins?

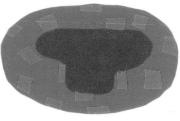

Match the pets to their homes.

Which pet would you like?

How many
red cars...
blue doors...
brown dogs...
yellow umbrellas?

28

29

Can you find these as well?

a flower

a red car